Poppy the P

Looking through the window of the cat basket, Poppy stared at the tiny house in front of her. She couldn't help feeling shocked. *This* was where she was going to live? What would Princess say if she saw it? The Siamese had told her that all pedigree cats lived in big houses, like Mrs Kent's . . .

Titles in Jenny Dale's KITTEN TALES™ series

All of Jenny Dale's KITTEN TALES books can
be ordered at your local bookshop or are
available by post from Book Service by Post
(tel: 01624 675137)

Poppy the Posh Kitten

by Jenny Dale

Illustrated by Susan Hellard

A Working Partners Book

MACMILLAN CHILDREN'S BOOKS

Special thanks to Narinder Dhami

First published 2001 by Macmillan Children's Books
a division of Macmillan Publishers Limited
20 New Wharf Road, London N1 9RR
Basingstoke and Oxford
www.panmacmillan.com

Associated companies throughout the world

Created by Working Partners Limited
London W6 0QT

ISBN 0 330 39733 8

3 5 7 9 8 6 4 2

A CIP catalogue record for this book is available from
the British Library.

Typeset by SX Composing DTP, Rayleigh, Essex
Printed and bound in Great Britain by Mackays of Chatham plc, Kent

Chapter One

"Poppy! What are you doing?"
Poppy jumped guiltily at the
sound of Princess's sharp miaow.
She wasn't doing *anything*, really.
She was out in the huge garden,
in the run which had been
specially built for Mrs Kent's cats.
Poppy was longing to explore the

rest of the garden. She'd been poking at the wire mesh with her paw to see if she could make a hole in it and get through.

"You were trying to get out of the run, weren't you?" Princess, a cream-and-chocolate coloured Siamese cat, strolled down the run towards Poppy. Her blue eyes were fixed accusingly on the fluffy white kitten.

"No, I wasn't, Princess!" Poppy mewed. Princess was very beautiful, with her silky coat and sparkling eyes. Even though she was a little scared of the bigger cat, Poppy hoped she would be just as beautiful when she grew up. Mrs Kent owned five show cats, including Poppy's mum,

Dorcas. But none of the cats had won as many cups, medals and rosettes as Princess.

"You *are* silly, Poppy," Princess sniffed, looking the kitten up and down. "Why on earth do you want to get out of the run? You're safe in here."

"I just wanted to have a look

around," Poppy miaowed.

"What, and meet some of those dirty, common cats who come into the garden sometimes?" Princess snapped. She sounded quite alarmed at the thought. "Just remember you're a *pedigree* cat, Poppy. A pedigree cat mustn't have anything to do with common old moggies – they're not as beautiful or as clever as us!"

"Yes, Princess," Poppy mewed obediently.

"You don't want to be like one of *those* cats," Princess went on, holding her chocolate-coloured nose in the air. "They live in tiny houses, not lovely big ones like Mrs Kent's, and they have to eat food out of *tins*!" She shuddered.

"It's disgusting!"

Poppy copied Princess and looked disgusted too. Dorcas was always telling Poppy that Princess was snooty, and not to take any notice of her. But Poppy couldn't help it. The Siamese was *so* beautiful, and she'd won *so* many competitions. Poppy wanted to be just like her.

"Those cats run about and climb trees and get all mussed up," Princess went on. She stretched out one leg, and delicately cleaned her toes. "And their owners don't care a bit! But *pedigree* owners like us to be clean and beautiful all the time, because they care about us so much."

Just then, Mrs Kent appeared at

the top of the run. "Poppy! Princess!" she called. "Dinner!"

"Oh, good," purred Princess. She walked off towards the house, her long tail swishing from side to side. "I hope it's fresh fish today."

Poppy ran after her, licking her lips. When she reached the kitchen, Mrs Kent was putting down five bowls of fish on the floor. Poppy went and tucked into the bowl next to her mum's.

"I hope that Princess hasn't been putting silly ideas into your head, Poppy," miaowed Dorcas in between mouthfuls.

"No, Mum," Poppy mewed back. But as she ate, Poppy thought about all those poor cats who had to eat horrible food that

came in tins. Yuck! She couldn't
help feeling sorry for them, even
though Princess said that they
were common. *I hope I don't ever
have to eat tinned food*, Poppy
thought to herself. It sounded
awful!

"I'm going to brush you now,
Poppy," Mrs Kent said, when the
kitten had cleaned her bowl. "Up
you come."

Poppy began to purr. She loved
being brushed and groomed. The
brush tickled and it left her fur all
fluffy and soft. She had never
been dirty in her life.

"Only common old moggies get
dirty," Princess had told Poppy.

And since then, Poppy had

done her very best to keep her thick, long-haired fur clean and beautiful.

"I've got a surprise for you, Poppy," Mrs Kent went on, as she brushed Poppy's already gleaming coat. "Lisa and her mum are coming to visit today."

Poppy's big blue eyes lit up. She loved Mrs Kent's granddaughter,

Lisa. Whenever Lisa came over, they always played lots of games together. And Lisa would brush Poppy's coat until she looked like a fluffy white cloud. "Brilliant!" she purred.

Just then, the doorbell rang. Poppy jumped off Mrs Kent's lap. "Is that Lisa now?" she miaowed excitedly. "Open the door, Mrs Kent!"

Mrs Kent went down the hall to the front door, and Poppy dashed after her. At least, Poppy was *going* to dash after her until she spotted Princess eyeing her sternly.

"Pedigree cats don't charge around all over the place like common old moggies do!"

Princess had told Poppy firmly.

So Poppy trotted calmly and coolly down the hall after Mrs Kent, even though she was so excited to see Lisa.

"Hello, Gran," said Lisa. She hurried in, followed by her mum, Mrs Martin. "Hello, Poppy!" And she picked the kitten up.

Poppy was already purring like an engine. She rubbed her head happily against Lisa's cheek.

"Have you told Poppy yet, Gran?" Lisa asked excitedly.

"Told me what?" Poppy miaowed, puzzled.

"You're coming to live with me and mum and Barney today, Poppy!" Lisa announced, her eyes shining. "You're going to be *my*

kitten! Isn't that brilliant?"

"Oh!" Poppy mewed. She'd
known, of course, that one day
she'd have to leave Mrs Kent's,
and go to a new home. But she'd
never *dreamed* she'd be going to
live with Lisa!

Mrs Kent turned to Lisa's mum
with a smile. "I'm glad that you
finally agreed to let Lisa have

Poppy," she said.

Mrs Martin laughed. "Well, as you know, we've already got Barney, and I thought two cats would be too much. But Lisa loves Poppy so much, I couldn't keep saying no!"

Mrs Kent nodded. "Yes, I know Poppy will be going to a good home," she said, stroking the kitten's fluffy head. "You *will* remember to brush her every day, won't you, Lisa?"

"Of course I will!" Lisa said.

"Don't worry, Lisa," Poppy mewed. "I'll make sure I stay clean and beautiful!"

Some of the other cats came over to see what was going on.

"So, my little Poppy is going to

a new home?" purred Dorcas, wrapping herself around Lisa's ankles.

Poppy looked down at her mum from Lisa's arms. "Yes, Mum!" she mewed. "I'll miss you, but isn't it exciting?"

Princess sat in the doorway, delicately washing her face with a chocolate-brown paw. "I bet your new home won't be as nice as this one!" she purred smugly.

"Don't you listen, Poppy," Dorcas miaowed firmly. "You'll be fine with Lisa."

Princess sniffed. "Well, just you remember all the things I've taught you, Poppy," she purred snootily. "You're a pedigree cat, and don't you forget it!"

Chapter Two

"Here we are, Poppy." Lisa lifted up the cat basket so that the kitten could see out of the car window. "This is your new home!"

Looking through the basket's window, Poppy stared at the tiny house in front of her. She couldn't help feeling shocked. *This* was where she was going to live? What would Princess say if she saw it? The Siamese had told her that all pedigree cats lived in big houses, like Mrs Kent's!

Poppy felt rather gloomy as Lisa carried her up the path to the front door. But she cheered up a bit when they went inside. Even though the house was small, it was warm and cosy. *Maybe it won't be too bad*, she told herself. *After all, even if the house is tiny, I'll be able to run around outside.*

Lisa put the cat basket down on the kitchen floor, then opened it. "Come on out, Poppy," she said happily.

Poppy stepped delicately out of

the basket and took a good look around. There was a cat flap in the back door, just like she was used to. The one at Mrs Kent's house led to the large run that all the cats played in. Poppy padded over to the door, and gave the flap a push with her head.

It didn't move.

"The cat flap's locked, Poppy," Lisa said. "You can't go out into the garden until you've had your injections."

Poppy looked up at Lisa, feeling puzzled. "Haven't you got a special run for me?" she mewed.

But as she stared through the clear plastic window in the cat flap, Poppy saw that the Martins' garden wasn't like Mrs Kent's at all. Lisa's gran had neat lawns and flowerbeds. This garden had long grass – some of it was taller than Poppy! And bushes, and big, shadowy trees . . .

Suddenly, a furry face looked right back at Poppy from the other side of the cat flap window! Poppy yowled with fright then rushed over to Lisa and ran up her jeans, into her arms. "Save, me, Lisa!" she mewed.

"Ow, ow!" Lisa cried, half laughing. "Poppy! It's OK! It's only Barney," she said, stroking the scared kitten.

"I'll let him in," said Mrs Martin, and she hurried over to the cat flap. She unlocked it and, at once, a young black-and-white tomcat tumbled through it.

"Hi," Barney miaowed, beaming up at Poppy. "I'm Barney! Who are you?"

Poppy, who was still clinging onto Lisa, stared down at Barney. He was *filthy*! His coat was more like black and grey than black and white! And he had leaves and bits of grass stuck to his coat as well! Poppy couldn't imagine what on *earth* Barney must have been doing to get in such a mess. He *did* look friendly though . . .

Seeing that her new kitten was no longer so nervous, Lisa put Poppy back down on the floor.

Barney came over to give Poppy a friendly sniff.

Poppy remembered what Princess had said. "I'm Poppy, the pedigree kitten," she mewed. "And *you* are not very clean!"

"Well, I've been playing outside," Barney miaowed cheerfully. "I can show you all the best places to play in the garden!"

"No, thank you," Poppy mewed snootily, putting her nose in the air just like Princess did.

Barney looked surprised. "Well, if you haven't had your injections yet, we can play in the house instead—"

"I don't *want* to play with you," Poppy hissed. Princess would be very proud of her, she thought. But even so, Poppy couldn't help feeling a bit guilty. Barney was only trying to be friendly.

Barney looked surprised. "Suit yourself," he meowed. Then his green eyes lit up as Lisa went over to one of the cupboards. "Oh, great – food!"

Poppy was feeling a bit peckish herself. So she trotted over to Lisa too. "Fresh fish is my favourite, Lisa," she mewed hungrily. "And I don't mind chicken, liver and steak too."

But what was that in Lisa's hand? Poppy could hardly believe her eyes. It was a *tin* – a tin of catfood!

"Mmm, that smells good!" purred Barney, as Lisa spooned some of the catfood into two bowls, then put them both on the kitchen floor. "Come on, Poppy – dig in."

"I can't eat *that*!" Poppy squeaked in dismay. She watched Barney begin to eat from one of the bowls. Then her tiny nose twitched in surprise. The food smelled quite nice. But what *would* Princess say if she knew that Poppy had been eating tinned food? She'd never speak to Poppy again!

"Oh well," snuffled Barney. "Can't let it go to waste." And he scoffed Poppy's bowlful as well as his own.

"Aren't you hungry, Poppy?" Lisa asked.

"Yes, I am," Poppy mewed miserably. "But I can't eat that

stuff. You'll have to give me some *proper* food!"

Barney trotted over to the cat flap. "Sure you don't want me to stay in and play with you?" he miaowed.

"Quite sure, thank you," Poppy mewed frostily.

Mrs Martin let Barney out again, and he disappeared into the overgrown garden.

Lisa picked Poppy up. "You'll soon settle in and get used to everything, Poppy," she said kindly, smoothing the kitten's fluffy coat.

Feeling more cheerful, Poppy snuggled down in Lisa's arms. She just had to remember that she was a special, pedigree cat, not a common moggy like Barney. And as long as she kept her coat clean and white and beautiful, everyone would be very proud of her.

Chapter Three

"*Barney*!" Poppy hissed crossly. "Get away from me!"

The black-and-white cat had just leaped out at Poppy from behind the TV. Her tail twitched angrily. Barney was just too rough!

Barney looked disappointed. "Come on, let's fight!" he

miaowed. "I won't hurt you."

"No, thank you," Poppy sniffed. She padded out of the living room, her nose in the air.

Poppy had been living with Lisa and Mrs Martin for a week now. And Barney was *always* trying to get her to play with him. How on earth was she supposed to keep her fluffy white coat nice and clean when Barney was such a nuisance? Poppy had decided to eat the tinned food, because there was nothing else, after all. But she was not going to get all dusty and dirty like Barney – no way!

Barney bounded after Poppy, playfully swiping at her plumy tail with his paw. "Where did Lisa take you this morning after breakfast?" he asked curiously.

"To the vet," Poppy mewed gloomily. "He stuck a needle in my neck, and it hurt!"

"Well, that means you've had all your injections. Now you'll be able to come and play outside!" Barney replied. He launched himself at her again. But Poppy side-stepped neatly, and Barney ended up in a tangled black-and-white heap on the hall rug.

"*Outside*?" Poppy repeated, her big blue eyes opening wide. She had forgotten all about that! She hurried over to the back door and stared through the cat flap window, her heart beating fast.

Lisa's garden looked very exciting. There were lots of places to explore, and lots of trees to climb, and—

A pedigree cat doesn't run about or climb trees . . . Poppy could hear Princess's snooty miaow again.

Poppy sat down and began to wash her paws – even though they didn't really need it. *What was I thinking of*? she asked herself glumly. Of course she wouldn't be able to do all those things. She had to keep herself clean and tidy, or Lisa wouldn't be proud of her any more. Princess had said that pedigree owners liked their cats to look beautiful all the time.

But to Poppy's surprise, Lisa came into the kitchen and opened the door. "Guess what, Poppy," she said. "We're going out to play in the garden!"

"Told you, Pops!" Barney miaowed eagerly. He shot out into the garden, calling, "Come on!"

Poppy sniffed. "I won't be going outside *that* much," she mewed. "And *don't* call me Pops!"

But standing in the doorway, Poppy couldn't help feeling excited. The interesting new smells made her whiskers twitch. She followed Lisa outside, onto the little patio. Her blue eyes darted from side to side.

The garden seemed much bigger now that Poppy was in it. The overgrown lawn was dotted with yellow flowers and filled with buzzing bees and fluttering butterflies. At the bottom of the garden, where the trees grew close together, the grass was very long. It looked really exciting.

"Go on, Poppy," Lisa said. "Go and explore."

Her heart beating fast, Poppy stepped carefully across the patio, towards the lawn. Then suddenly, Barney popped out from behind a bush and made her jump.

"Barney!" Poppy hissed, her fur all ruffled. Then she stared at the black-and-white cat. He had grass seeds and bits of leaves stuck in his furry coat already.

Poppy stayed where she was – it was nice and clean.

"OK, we'll have a game here then," said Lisa. She took a little rubber ball out of her pocket, and rolled it along the patio.

Poppy knew this game. It was one she could play, and still stay tidy! She chased after the ball, and stopped it with her paw.

"Good girl!" Lisa smiled, and Poppy felt very pleased with

herself. But she couldn't help sneaking a look at Barney. He was romping through the long grass, chasing butterflies. He was having a great time.

"Well, so am I!" Poppy told herself firmly.

Then Lisa rolled the ball a bit too hard. It went off the patio and

into the long grass.

"I can't get that, Lisa," Poppy mewed sadly. "I'll get all messy!"

"I'll get it, Poppy," Lisa called. She went off to find the ball.

Barney was now rolling over and over on the path, stretching himself in the sun, and getting dustier and dirtier. "Come and have a roll on the path, Poppy!" he purred loudly. "It feels great!"

"You must be joking," Poppy mewed snootily. "Look how dirty you are!" But she couldn't help thinking that Barney was having a *much* better time than she was.

Chapter Four

"Shall I or shan't I?" Poppy
mewed to herself, as she sat in
front of the cat flap. It was open
all day now that Poppy had had
her injections. But Poppy hadn't
been out by herself yet.

Poppy was bored. It was
Monday afternoon, so Lisa was at

school and Mrs Martin was at work. Barney had been out in the garden all day because the sun was shining. Not that she cared *where* Barney was, Poppy told herself firmly. But it *was* a bit lonely in the house with no one else there.

Poppy took a deep breath, and began to climb through the flap. Next moment, she was outside on the sunny patio. "I did it!" she miaowed proudly.

"Hey, look at that!" someone called. "What is it?"

Poppy looked round sharply. Three cats were sitting in a row on top of the fence, looking down at her, their tails swinging. One of them was Barney, but Poppy hadn't seen the other two before. One was a big ginger tom, and the other was a small tabby.

"I beg your pardon," Poppy mewed sniffily, "but were you talking to *me*?"

"Oh, it's a *real* cat!" the ginger tom howled to his friends. "I thought it was a cuddly toy!"

"She looks snooty," the smaller tabby miaowed disapprovingly.

"Leave her alone, you two," warned Barney. "Poppy, this is Henry and this is Lily. They're mates of mine."

"I might have known," Poppy sniffed. She sat down on the patio with her back to them, her tail twitching crossly.

"She thinks she's too good for *us*!" Henry miaowed. The three cats jumped down from the fence. "She's Poppy the *Posh* Kitten!"

"Those pedigree cats always think they're better than us," Lily spat.

"Poppy's OK," Barney miaowed. "Come on, let's play Catch-the-Leaf!"

Poppy couldn't help sneaking a quick look. Barney, Henry and Lily were running around in the long grass. It looked like they were having loads of fun as they pounced and leaped around in the sunshine.

Suddenly, Princess's miaow popped into Poppy's mind . . . *A pedigree cat mustn't have anything*

to do with common old moggies!
*They're not as beautiful or as clever
as we are!*

No, but they have a lot more fun!
Poppy thought gloomily, as
Barney, Henry and Lily flopped
down on the path and began to
roll around in the dust.

"What shall we do now?"
Barney panted.

"Let's climb one of the trees,"
Henry suggested. "Let's see who
can climb right up to that big
branch over there!"

Poppy looked at the tree Henry
was talking about. It was one of
the tallest in the garden. The big
branch was about halfway up.
It looked almost impossible to
get to.

"What are *you* looking at, Poppy the Posh?" Henry miaowed rudely. "Are *you* going to have a go?"

"Pedigree cats are useless at climbing!" Lily sniffed scornfully.

Suddenly Poppy was fed up with everyone telling her what she couldn't do. She was fed up with sitting on the patio and keeping clean and neat. And most of all, she was fed up with being Poppy the Posh Kitten!

"I *can* climb up there!" she mewed loudly. "In fact, I'll climb up there right now!"

Chapter Five

Poppy hadn't meant to say that at
all. In fact, she was even more
shocked by what she'd just said
than Barney, Henry and Lily
were. The three cats sat staring at
her, their eyes as round as
marbles.

"You don't mean that, Poppy!"

Barney miaowed. He sounded a bit worried.

"'Course she doesn't," Lily scoffed. "She's just showing off."

"As if Poppy the Posh Kitten could climb up there," Henry added. "She couldn't even climb onto a chair!"

"Right!" Her tail ramrod straight, Poppy marched furiously across the patio, and onto the grass. She headed for the tree and stopped at the bottom of it. "Now you'll see whether pedigree cats can climb or not!"

"This should be fun!" Henry remarked. He settled himself down on the path and tucked his paws underneath him.

Poppy looked up at the tree and

gulped. It was *very* high. And she didn't even know how to start. Her heart sank. She'd made a fool of herself in front of Barney and his friends.

"If you climb up that little tree there, you can get onto the fence." Barney was suddenly beside her, whispering in her ear. "Then you'll be able to get into the lower branches of the big tree."

"Thanks," Poppy mewed.

"Take it slowly and don't look down," Barney went on, giving her a gentle nudge. "It's not as difficult as it looks. Good luck!"

Knowing that Barney thought she could do it made Poppy feel a bit braver. She took a deep breath, and set off up the little tree towards the fence.

Climbing the little tree was difficult enough. It swayed in the breeze, and Poppy swayed with it. But she clung on tightly with her claws. And soon, to her delight, she was scrambling onto the top of the fence. She'd done it!

"Well done, Poppy!" Barney miaowed, as she padded carefully

along the fence towards the lowest branches of the big tree.

"Huh! That was nothing," Henry said scornfully. "That was the *easy* bit!"

But Poppy wasn't going to stop now. The big tree didn't look *quite* so big now that she was on top of the fence. And the branch didn't look quite so high.

She set off along the lower branches, placing her paws carefully and delicately as she made her way up the tree. Poppy had never dreamed that she might be good at climbing. But because she was very sure-footed she was doing rather well.

"I'm good at climbing!" Poppy miaowed gleefully, as she went

even higher. "I'm really, really
good at climbing – OH!"
Suddenly, her paw slipped and
she almost lost her footing.

"Be careful, Poppy!" Barney
called anxiously.

Poppy stopped for a moment,
her heart beating fast. Then she
went on. The big branch was
getting very close now. One more

step, and—

"Look at me!" Poppy purred triumphantly. "I made it!"

"See, Henry?" Barney was jumping around excitedly at the bottom of the tree. "I told you she could do it!"

"She's still got to come down yet," Henry muttered, looking rather uncomfortable.

Coming down was a bit tricky too. But by now Poppy was so confident that there was no stopping her. She strolled from branch to branch, swung herself down onto the fence and then slid casually down the little tree.

"Well done, Poppy!" Barney said. "You were brilliant!"

"You're a really good climber,

Poppy," Lily added admiringly.

"Thanks." Poppy looked at Henry. "What do *you* think, Henry?" she mewed.

"OK, OK!" Henry miaowed reluctantly. "You're not bad for a pedigree cat."

"Come on, Pops." Barney swiped at Poppy's ear playfully. "Let's have a game of Hide-and-Seek!" And he dashed off towards the trees at the bottom of the garden. Lily and Henry followed.

Poppy stood there staring after them for a moment. She could hear Princess saying very clearly, *A pedigree cat* never *plays with common old moggies*!

"Oh, shut up, Princess!" Poppy miaowed loudly, and she

scampered off after her new friends.

While Poppy was playing in the garden, Lisa was on her way home from school. Her mum was at work today, so Lisa's gran had come to collect her.

"I can't wait to see Poppy again!" Mrs Kent said eagerly, as they walked home. "I'm so glad she's settled in well with you."

Lisa nodded. "Although I think she's having problems getting used to Barney!" she said, smiling.

"Well, Poppy *is* a pedigree kitten," Mrs Kent pointed out. She unlocked the Martins' front door. "Maybe Barney's a bit rough for her."

"Maybe," Lisa agreed doubtfully, as they went inside. "Poppy! Poppy, where are you?" she called.

But there was no sign of the kitten.

"She must have gone outside," Lisa said at last.

"Oh dear, I hope Poppy's all right in the garden on her own," Mrs Kent said anxiously, as they went outside. "She was always kept inside the run when she lived with me."

"Poppy?" Lisa called, looking round the garden.

Suddenly a white streak of fur shot out of the undergrowth at the bottom of the garden, with

Barney in hot pursuit.

"Hello, Lisa!" Poppy mewed chirpily. "Hello, Mrs Kent!" And that was all she had time to say before Barney jumped on her, and they both rolled over and over on the dusty path.

"*Poppy*!" Mrs Kent shrieked, horrified. "What's *happened* to you?"

Chapter Six

Poppy had never heard Mrs Kent shout before. She jumped to her paws in surprise. So did Barney. Henry and Lily, who were behind them, crept away into the long grass.

"What's the matter?" Poppy mewed. Why were Mrs Kent and

Lisa staring at her like that?

Then she looked down at herself. Her beautiful white coat was matted and covered with sticky grass seeds, and it was streaked with dirt and dust. Poppy could hardly believe what she'd done.

"Oh, Poppy!" Lisa's gran was so

shocked, she could hardly speak. "Your beautiful coat! It's ruined!"

Poppy hung her dusty little head. "I'm sorry, Lisa," she mewed. "I didn't mean to get all dirty. We were having so much fun, I didn't even notice. I'll never do it again!"

Barney gave her a nudge. "But, Poppy, we had loads of fun, and Henry and Lily really like you now!" he miaowed. "They're going to come round to play again tomorrow."

"They are?" Poppy brightened up a bit, but only for a minute. Then she was glum again. How could she have fun with her new friends, but still keep herself clean and beautiful for Lisa?

But when Poppy looked at her owner again, she couldn't believe her eyes. Lisa was *smiling*.

"Oh, Poppy!" Lisa laughed, scooping her kitten into her arms. "You look so funny! And cuter than ever!"

Funny? Cute? Poppy cheered up immediately. Lisa wasn't angry with her after all!

"But, Lisa, *look* at her coat!" Mrs Kent groaned.

"I don't care, Gran!" Lisa replied firmly, giving the kitten a hug. "I love Poppy *whatever* she looks like!"

"And I love you too, Lisa!" Poppy purred happily. She rubbed her head against Lisa's chin. All this time she'd been trying so hard to keep herself clean and beautiful. And Lisa didn't even *care*! Poppy felt very relieved indeed.

Lisa grinned as she carried her kitten into the house. "It looks like Poppy had fun playing with Barney," she said.

"Yes, I did," Poppy mewed. "But he cheats at Hide-and-Seek!"

"Ooh, I do not!" Barney yowled, as he bounded into the house behind them. Mrs Kent followed, still looking a bit worried.

Lisa fetched Poppy's brush and began to groom her coat. The kitten purred loudly as Barney helped out by giving her a few friendly licks too.

After ten minutes, Poppy's coat

was fluffy and white again. "I like being clean and beautiful," she miaowed to Barney. "But it's fun to get messy too!"

"Look, Gran." Lisa turned to Mrs Kent. "Poppy's coat is fine, really it is."

"Yes, I can see that," Mrs Kent admitted reluctantly.

"I'm starving!" Barney miaowed.

Poppy realised *she* was hungry too.

Both cats twined themselves around Lisa's legs as she opened a tin of catfood and spooned it into their bowls.

"Yum yum!" Poppy licked her lips, and began to tuck in.

Lisa's gran could hardly believe

her eyes. "I didn't think Poppy would like tinned food," she said.

"Neither did I!" Poppy mewed. "But I'm getting used to it. It's really quite tasty – and you can tell Princess I said so!"

"Do you want that?" Barney asked. He'd finished his own bowl, and was looking hungrily at what was left in Poppy's.

"Yes, I do, greedy-guts!" Poppy replied, giving him a playful swipe with her paw.

"Well, Lisa, Poppy *does* seem very happy," Mrs Kent said, smiling. "I'm glad."

"I *love* it here," Poppy miaowed, then she yawned widely. "Time for a nap, I think."

"Lisa's bed, or the living room rug?" Barney asked.

Poppy thought for a moment. "Lisa's bed!" she replied. And the two cats galloped upstairs. They jumped onto Lisa's bed and curled up together in one tight, furry ball.

"This little house is really cosy," Poppy yawned, her eyelids already drooping. "There's lots of nice, warm places to curl up and have a snooze."

"I thought you said it was too small," Barney teased her, yawning himself.

"I was as snooty as Princess then!" Poppy replied sleepily. "But I'm not Poppy the Posh Kitten any more. From now on, I'm Poppy the *Pet* Kitten!"